P9-DHO-901

The Dragon and George

by James Cressey and Tamasin Cole

Prentice-Hall, Inc.
Englewood Cliffs, N.J.

Copyright © 1977 by A & C Black Ltd.
First American edition published 1979 by Prentice-Hall, Inc.
All rights reserved. No part of this book may be
reproduced in any form or by any means, except for
the inclusion of brief quotations in a review,
without permission in writing from the publisher.
Printed in the United States of America
1 2 3 4 5 6 7 8 9 10
Library of Congress Cataloging in Publication Data
Cressey, James.
The dragon and George.

  SUMMARY: A contemporary spoof on the story of
Saint George and the dragon, in which the last
English dragon and a modern day George conspire
to please the public.
  [1. Dragons—Fiction] I. Cole, Tamasin.
II. Title.
PZ7.C8643Dr 1979   [E]   79-15751
ISBN 0-13-219154-7

Once there was a town at the top of a hill. The people who lived in the town did not like dragons. Over the years their knights had slain all of them but one.

The last dragon lived in a cave at the bottom
of the hill.

This hill was not very far from the winding
road leading up to the town.

Like all dragons, he breathed fire from his mouth.
The people of the town hated him and his fiery
breath. "It is exactly like living at the top of a
volcano," they said. And they ordered the knights to
go out every day to fight the dragon.

But the last dragon, in spite of his fiery breath, did
not like to fight at all. He was a very gentle dragon
and tried hard never to hurt the knights.

The knights, some of whom had fought the **first** dragon the town ever had, were old men by this time. They did not like fighting the dragon at all, any more than he like fighting them. But they had to do what the townspeople wanted.

"Dragons and their caves belong in museums, not near towns," the people said. And so the fighting continued every day, even though the knights and the dragon were tired of the whole thing.

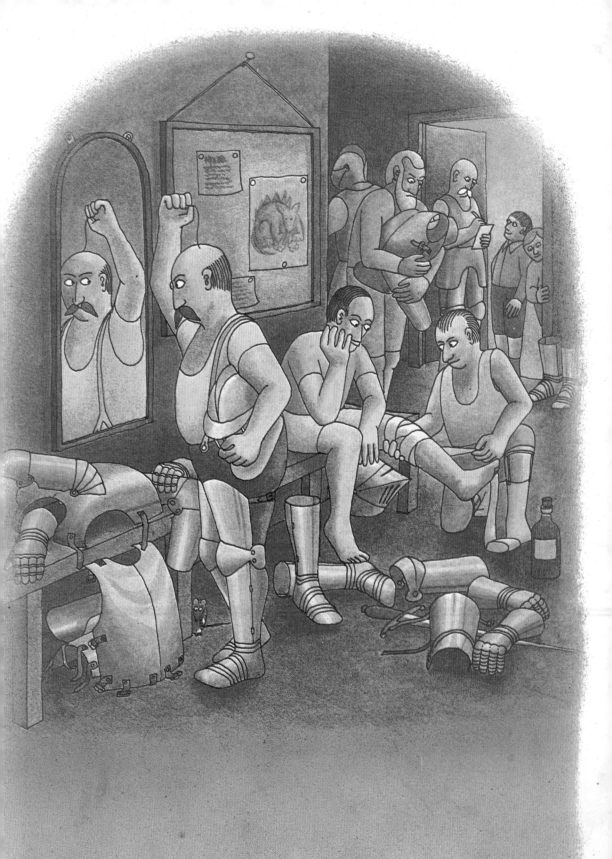

Then one morning, winding its way towards the
town at the top of the hill, came George's Travelling
Circus. There were elephants and giraffes and fierce
lions and tigers. There was a fat lady and clowns
and acrobats.

And they were all led by a dancing bear. The dragon
watched the circus go by. He began to think.

By now the dragon was very good at swallowing swords and was getting very bored. After seeing the circus that day and having an idea, he stayed up all night trying to work it out and wondering if it would succeed.

The next day he invited George the Circus Owner to his cave for supper. After they had eaten a delicious meal they talked of the plan. George liked the dragon and approved of his plan. He believed it would work.

So George held a meeting with all the knights and
told them of the plan. They listened very carefully
and said they approved of the plan.

Then George arranged a tournament. First he told
the town crier to announce it all over the town:
George the Circus Owner to fight the Fire-breathing
Dragon! A fight to the death! The town would be rid
of the dragon for ever! This is what the town crier
was to say.

When the great day came, people gathered from the town on the hill. And they gathered from towns and villages for miles around as well.

The dragon looked as fierce as he could. He looked so frightening that even though the knights knew all about the plan, they shivered and shook so that their armor rattled.

Then George borrowed a suit of armor and a sword from one of the knights and went forth to meet the dragon. The townspeople thought he was very brave and shouted to encourage him.

The dragon pretended to fight like an angry dragon, to make it look hard for George. Sometimes the dragon chased George and sometimes George chased the dragon.

At last George put his sword down the throat of the
dragon, who fell to the ground, The townspeople
cheered and clapped loudly.

The knights felt brave enough to come close to the dragon and tickle his feet. He did not twitch or giggle at all, and this proved to everyone that the dragon was dead. The knights were happy because there were no more dragons to fight.

The townspeople were happy because they were rid of the terrifying dragon with the fiery breath. They were grateful to George.

George was happy because he could move on with his circus and travel to far-off places.

The last dragon was happy because he loved swallowing swords and breathing out fire on all the crowds who came to watch George's Travelling Circus.